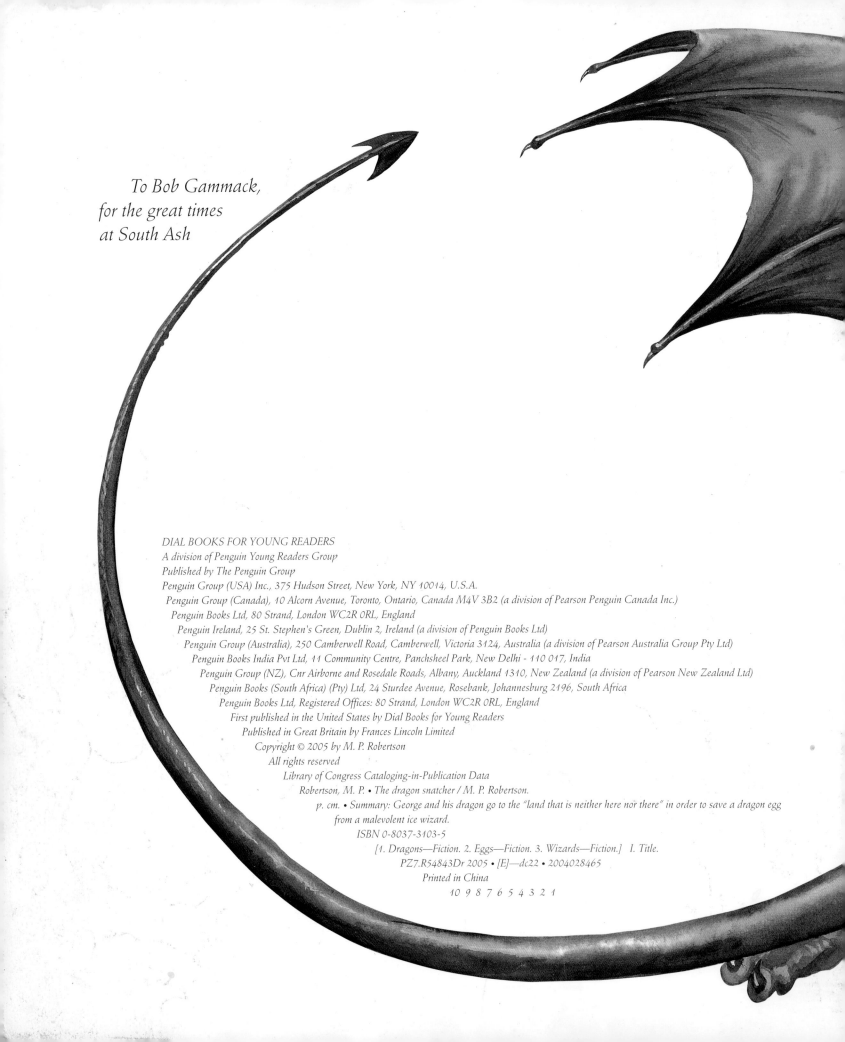

To Bob Gammack,
for the great times
at South Ash

DIAL BOOKS FOR YOUNG READERS
A division of Penguin Young Readers Group
Published by The Penguin Group
Penguin Group (USA) Inc., 375 Hudson Street, New York, NY 10014, U.S.A.
Penguin Group (Canada), 10 Alcorn Avenue, Toronto, Ontario, Canada M4V 3B2 (a division of Pearson Penguin Canada Inc.)
Penguin Books Ltd, 80 Strand, London WC2R 0RL, England
Penguin Ireland, 25 St. Stephen's Green, Dublin 2, Ireland (a division of Penguin Books Ltd)
Penguin Group (Australia), 250 Camberwell Road, Camberwell, Victoria 3124, Australia (a division of Pearson Australia Group Pty Ltd)
Penguin Books India Pvt Ltd, 11 Community Centre, Panchsheel Park, New Delhi - 110 017, India
Penguin Group (NZ), Cnr Airborne and Rosedale Roads, Albany, Auckland 1310, New Zealand (a division of Pearson New Zealand Ltd)
Penguin Books (South Africa) (Pty) Ltd, 24 Sturdee Avenue, Rosebank, Johannesburg 2196, South Africa
Penguin Books Ltd, Registered Offices: 80 Strand, London WC2R 0RL, England
First published in the United States by Dial Books for Young Readers
Published in Great Britain by Frances Lincoln Limited
Copyright © 2005 by M. P. Robertson
All rights reserved
Library of Congress Cataloging-in-Publication Data
Robertson, M. P. • The dragon snatcher / M. P. Robertson.
p. cm. • Summary: George and his dragon go to the "land that is neither here nor there" in order to save a dragon egg
from a malevolent ice wizard.
ISBN 0-8037-3103-5
[1. Dragons—Fiction. 2. Eggs—Fiction. 3. Wizards—Fiction.] I. Title.
PZ7.R54843Dr 2005 • [E]—dc22 • 2004028465
Printed in China
10 9 8 7 6 5 4 3 2 1

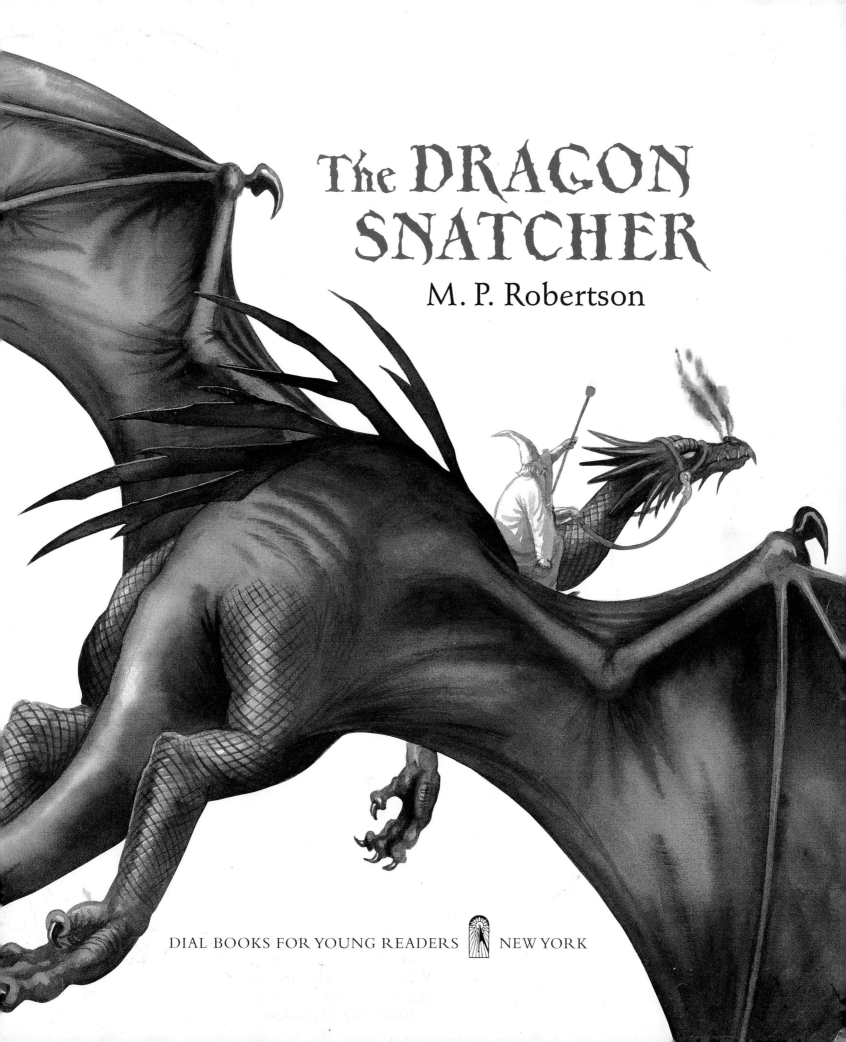

The DRAGON SNATCHER

M. P. Robertson

DIAL BOOKS FOR YOUNG READERS NEW YORK

utside, snow lay deep on the ground.
George nestled among his books.
It was a night to be wrapped warmly in the
pages of a story. But as George was reading,
he was disturbed by a commotion from
the chicken house.

George peered out of his window.
Looking up at him was his dragon.
He had a worried look in his yellow eyes.
George threw a blanket around his shoulders
and climbed out onto the dragon's neck.
He clung tightly as they were whisked
on the North Wind to a land that was
neither Here nor There.

Over lofty peaks they soared, until George saw
a dark castle that cut through the ice like a shard
of flint. The dragon landed silently and hid
beneath the drawbridge. George knew it wasn't
only the cold that made his dragon shiver.
There was something evil within.

George entered the castle alone.
He came to a courtyard where a soot-black dragon
stood guard. Keeping to the shadows,
George sneaked past.

He found a staircase that wound its way
up through the heart of the castle. At the top
of the stairs was a heavy wooden door.
George heaved it open.

He couldn't believe what he found inside—
shelves and shelves of frost-covered eggs. Each was
carefully labeled, from *The Red-Crested Ridgeback*
to *The Horny Cave Dweller.* They were dragon eggs!
    There was only one empty space left to fill.
It was labeled:

The Lesser-Spotted
Red Crest
— extremely rare —

Suddenly George was startled by a noise on the stairs.
He hid quickly behind a large egg.

An old wizard with a beard of frost entered the room.
A shiver ran through George as the air became icy cold.

"Only one more to find," the wizard cackled.
"Then I will rid the land of these cursed creatures."

He stared into an orb of ice and began to
mumble strange incantations. In the center of the orb
George could see the mountains surrounding the castle.
The wizard searched the mountains looking into every
nook and cranny. On top of the highest peak was
a twisted tree. Among its branches was a dragon's nest,
and in the nest was a glowing, orange egg.

"There you are, my little beauty," hissed the wizard.
"Soon my egg collection will be complete!"

The wizard ran down the stairs into the courtyard
and mounted the black dragon. George leaned
out of the window and whistled for his dragon.
As he flew in front of the window, George
leaped onto his dragon's back.

They followed the black dragon at a distance.
Soon George spotted the twisted tree and—oh, no!
The wizard was crawling onto a branch toward
the dragon egg.
But George had a plan. Using his blanket as a net,
he snatched the egg from the wizard's icy clutches.

Then the chase began! A ball of fire came
whistling past George's ear and crashed
into the mountainside. The black dragon
was belching fire at them.

George's dragon flitted to and fro trying
to avoid the fireballs, but he misjudged a turn
and crashed into the face of a mountain.

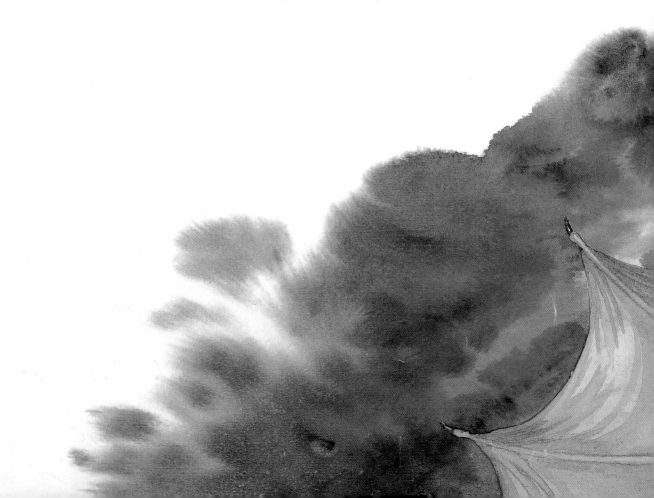

Luckily, George and his dragon landed softly in the snow, but the egg fell from the blanket. George watched as it rolled down the mountain and landed at the wizard's feet.

"It's mine!" said the wizard, holding the egg aloft.

But the egg began to glow as if there was a fire inside. It burned hotter and hotter until it was too hot for the wizard to hold. The egg was hatching!

The wizard looked on in disbelief as a tiny red dragon emerged. Then he sank to his knees, picking up pieces of shell.

"The last egg," he sobbed. "It's ruined!"

The baby dragon was looking at the wizard
with love in his eyes—chirruping like a chick.

"He thinks you're his mother," said George.

"I'm not your mother, you pathetic little creature!"
said the wizard.

But as his cruel glare met the bright yellow
eyes of the baby dragon, the wizard saw
the love that glowed within.
The ice that had frozen
his heart began to melt.

Back at the castle, the wizard's icy spell
had been broken. And as a new warmth filled
the egg-room, a wondrous thing happened!

The wizard led the baby dragon toward the castle.
He'll make a good mother, thought George.
And as he and his dragon flew over the castle,
a rainbow of newly hatched dragons filled the sky.
George headed for home, happy that once again
dragons would fly free in the land that is neither
Here nor There.